D0868682

A TIME
FOR
EVERYTHING:

The Celebration of Life

"For everything there is a season, and a time for every matter under heaven:

    a time to be born, and a time to die;
    a time to plant, and a time to pluck up what is planted;
    a time to kill, and a time to heal;
    a time to break down, and a time to build up;
    a time to weep, and a time to laugh;
    a time to mourn, and a time to dance;
    a time to cast away stones, and a time to gather stones together;
    a time to embrace, and a time to refrain from embracing;
    a time to seek, and a time to lose;
    a time to keep, and a time to cast away;
    a time to rend, and a time to sew;
    a time to keep silence, and a time to speak;
    a time to love, and a time to hate;
    a time for war, and a time for peace."

Ecclesiastes 3:1-8

THE CELEBRATION OF LIFE

The church is a community of celebration. At times it has lost the capacity and forgotten the need to celebrate life. We have experienced such a time in recent history. Only now are we recovering the celebrational dimension of the Christian community. We are finding the will to understand and perceive the deeper meanings of significant events and common ventures. In search of soul we are discovering life coming alive and calling for celebration. Christian celebration is the "sounding forth" of meanings found in encounter with life. To celebrate life Christianly is to receive all of life as a gift ... to receive it with gratitude and responsibility ... to appropriate it likewise with gratitude and responsibility.

This is a book of celebration. It is an attempt to convey in words the celebrations of a particular community -- Lake Shore Baptist Church in Waco, Texas. Some of the celebrations have been shared by the whole community. Others have remained personal prior to "going public" in this volume.

These writings are both personal and representative. They were born of the experience of the individuals who penned them. They were and are shared because they re-present the common humanity which is ours -- struggles and thrills ... sadness and gladness ... questions and affirmations ... worship and work ... faith and fear ... discouragement and hope -- all the things we celebrate as life. It is with "fear and trembling" that we share some of our "sounding forths."

A TIME FOR EVERYTHING

A Time To Begin

"Hear, O Israel: the Lord our God is one Lord; and you shall love the Lord your God with all your heart, and with all your soul, and with all your might."

The coming of a new year brings to the Community of Faith a new occasion for inventory ... a new challenge to order and reorder life. And to do it according to priorities that affirm the meaning of the Gospel and embody the way of the Christ.

The first three selections were written as theme interpretations designed to call the community to worship and to call our lives to commitment on the edge of a new year. They were printed on the front of the Sunday worship bulletins -- and incorporated into the sermons on three successive Sundays in January.

The beginning of a new year is a time for personal inventory, too. It is a time to look backward and to look forward ... to give thanks for the past ... to receive the present ... to shape the future. "Reflections on 1967" and "The Light In the Window" were both written on the verge of a new year.

Tend the garden, name the animals, subdue the earth,
                                              God said
And man did as God had said,
                     and more
                               He went for the moon
                     and made it!
What is man, that marvelous creature
                that does what God commands and more?

And the universe he probes, whose mystery he strips away,
                     What shall we say of it
The miracle of the moon is
                     no more
That yellow ball has become another place to go
                               another thing to do
                               another land to inhabit
                                    another planet to corrupt

For Man the Master of outer space
                               has yet to tame inner space
Man the Knower of all things
                               is to himself unknown
Man the Conqueror of every living thing (plant and animal)
                     cannot live at peace with his own kind
Man the Manipulator of the mystery of distant planets
                     finds listening to himself and his brother
                     the hardest work of all

Could it be
          that he who is winning the race to the moon
                     is losing the human race?

What does it profit to gain the whole universe
                               and lose soul?

                               Deryl Fleming

2

Going, grabbing, groping
      Wanting desperately to be liked
Give a little here
      Give a little there
Make this compromise, then that, and the other
      Until at last the goal is reached
Then comes the reward
      The gnawing of nothingness, the crisis of emptiness
Is it better to be liked than to BE?

Seeking, struggling, striving
      Needing terribly to be important
Join the "right" club
      Follow the "in" group
Do the things that one must do to become Somebody
      Until at last you arrive on Status Street
Then comes the discovery
      That one is merely a collection of other people's
      expectations
Is it better to be important than to BE?

What is recognition,
            if one can no longer recognize himself
      a promotion,
            if one has forfeited integrity
      status,
            if one has sold his selfhood
      a title,
            if there is no person behind it
      belonging,
            if there is no BE-ing

What does it profit to gain worlds of recognition
                              and lose soul?

                              Deryl Fleming

Money, money, money,
                    what money can do
It can use a man
                    or be used by him
It can make a man grateful
                    or greedy
It can buy medicine
                    but it can't buy health
It can express love
                    or the lack of it
It can come and it can go
                    so fast
It can free a man from debt
                    or plunge him deeper into it
It can talk
                    or keep a man from talking
It can fill a wallet
                    or empty a heart
It can enrich life
                    or impoverish it
It can put a man in business
                    or out of business
It can be beautiful
                    or ugly
It can serve God
                    or be god
Money, money, money,
                    what man can do with money
What does it profit to gain all the money
                    and lose soul?

                    Deryl Fleming

REFLECTIONS ON 1967

It has been a memorable year.

God has made Himself known to me in a new and deeper way --

through communion with Him and conversation with those He has chosen as "means of grace."

During 1967 I have spent more time alone -- and yet, at the same time, more time with large groups of people -- than any other year in sixteen years of marriage. I have been forced to ask myself the question -- "Who am I?"--

> a lawyer's wife?
> a mayor's wife?
> a hunter's wife?
> Jeff's mother?
> Jerry's mother?
> Jack's mother?
> a choir director?
> a community volunteer?
> a frustrated social worker?
> one who seeks approval more than accomplishment?

And to each I have answered "Yes" -- a little and then again, at times, a lot of each of these roles.

So -- at this point in my pilgrimage -- as I search for identity and fulfillment (like so many of the forty-ish women of our day), I must remember anew -- and *never* forget -- that I am one of *God's children.* And He has given me the "gift of life" -- with that gift stamped THROUGH JESUS CHRIST WITH LOVE (defined: FORGIVEN AND FREE TO BECOME).

It is "Good News" -- and as I accept His gift anew and afresh
My goal for '68 must be to offer myself as "means of grace" --
Knowing that many times I will stumble and fall - and yet, at
the same time, knowing that gift -- "to become" -- THROUGH
REPENTANCE is available to help me "become" --

NOT the musician OR the beautiful music,
   BUT THE INSTRUMENT
NOT the artist OR the painting,
   BUT THE BRUSH AND OILS
NOT the writer OR the profound utterance,
   BUT THE QUILL
NOT the power-plant OR the bright light,
   BUT THE POWER LINE
NOT the root OR the flower,
   BUT THE STEM
NOT asking for the blueprint,
   BUT for TODAY'S ASSIGNMENT

"Lord, make me an *instrument* of Thy peace."

Barbara Johnston

THE LIGHT IN THE WINDOW

Oh no, God! Not another year!
    This one's been so dreary and full of disappointments
Assassinations, murders, riots, endless monotonous repetition
    Not 1969 — I'm not ready for it.

Until I see the light in the window—
    The window next door, my neighbor's window
The man who's been dying of cancer for four years,
    Who only this year quit work to fight full-time his quiet
        battle with destiny

In and out of the hospital six times
    Up and down — pneumonia, flu — nearly lethal to someone
        already as ill as he
And never once losing his sense of humor —
    Still trying, hoping, smiling — still *wanting* to live

And I pray,
    "I'm sorry God
        I'll try again
            Surely I can make it another day."

Beverly Hill

A Time for Children

"Truly, I say to you, unless you turn and become like children, you will never enter the Kingdom of heaven."

Matthew 18:3

The enduring newness of life often comes from the newer lives among us -- our children. How many times the Word of God comes to us through a child. And it calls all of us to recovery of child-likeness. A new year is liable to begin in the middle of a year if you listen to the words and ways of a child.

The following prayer and poems were written by mothers who heard God speak through their children. "Happiness Is" and "Growing Up" were written by two of our younger ones in a Bible study class. "Pure Joy" reflects the excitement of one of our grandmothers. "Motherly Love" and "A Mother's Prayer" reflect the motherly concerns and hopes of the two mothers who wrote them and of all mothers who read them. "Being A Mother Is" is a collage of feelings that belong to mothers.

A PRAYER

God ... my own sins make me sick ...

My life has missed the mark so many times in so many ways ...

And now ... despair and self-pity are the "blue devils" that haunt me ...

Too often ... like last week ... I just feel like throwing in the towel ...

And God ... sometimes, I even feel like Nietsche ... and I want to run through the streets, shreiking ... God is dead ... Life is a rat race ... to hell with the whole mess ...

But then ... that note came in the mail ...

And, that call came from a friend ...

And, I came home one night, dog tired, hungry, lonely ... and as I walked in the door of a kitchen full of dirty dishes ...

My little girl threw her arms around me and said ... "Mommy, I like you a lot."

And, I heard you God ... you were right there ...

And, I prayed then ... and I'm praying now ...

Forgive me, Lord, for doubting

That you can help me be what you are calling me to be ...

IN SPITE OF EVERYTHING.

Amen.

Minnie Herring

LOVE TEXTURES

Morning voice calling "Mommy"
    Tinkling cascades of innocent laughter
Spat spat of bare feet fleeing
    Tiny grasping hands seeking refuge

Silken lashes brushing curved cheeks
    Pudgy tears poised to plunge
Tousled dreamer slumbering peacefully --
    Memories to save for a later day.

Beverly Hill

FOUR YEARS OLD

"God's phone number," he said;
Would I look it up? He had something important to say.
When I told him the line was open and free,
He exulted, Even I can pray?"

Donna McMullen

EARLY MORNING

Phillip is five, every inch alive, Running, climbing, rolling,
    yelling.
After a rain he watched birds bathing and saw the leap of a
    furry-tailed squirrel.
"What are you doing, Phillip?"
"Just looking at things, just loving the world."

Donna McMullen

HAPPINESS IS

Happiness is an "A" on report cards.

Happiness is visiting someone sick.

Happiness is a brand new pet dog, especially dachshunds.

Happiness is knowing God loves you, even if you're always being mean.

Happiness is getting a new neighbor.

Happiness is what you like, not what makes someone else happy.

Happiness is something different to each and every person.

If you like to go shopping, then that's happiness for you.

Most people like lots of things

If you see someone who is sad, try to cheer 'um up.

It may turn out to be happiness for you!

Susan Brister

GROWING UP

Growing up is having good and bad times
Happy and sad times
It is full of grief and sorrow
Also of thinking of tomorrow

Growing up is discovering a bee can sting
Also, that a bird has wings
And thinking of things to do
When little sister bothers you

Growing up is full of surprises
And sometimes full of winning prizes
It is full of runny noses
Also of bright spring roses

Kathy Casner

PURE JOY

Put away the bric-a-brac,
Latch the cupboard doors,
Search for fallen pin or tack,
Sweep and scrub the floors,
Take a pill to calm my nerves
And one to set me humming,
Store up rest and sleep reserves--
My little grandson's coming!

Penny Edens

MOTHERLY LOVE

Children, I'd like for my life to be
A pretty picture for you to see;
One you'll view and be able to tell
The pattern to pick to stay happy and well.
But, dears, I'm clothed in such human thread
That I'd not have you follow the path I have tread.
Instead, I'd remind you, my intentions are God-ward,
And pray in your lives, that Christ is your Lord.

Donna McMullen

A MOTHER'S PRAYER

Lord God,
What would you do --
If you had a child in the middle of a hurricane watch?
If you had a child in the "wild blue yonder"?
If you had a child surrounded by hippies?
If you had a child who's just come home from a fight?

Well, that's where I am.
And I feel lost and lonely and desperate and insecure --
More than that, I feel utterly inadequate -- and little -- and
    unloved

And I *know you* love me, God --
But, sometimes, I need so pitifully to feel human love.

Yet I have so much in the treasures you've given me --
The budding self-realization in one,
The tender empathy in another,
The vulnerable earnestness in one,
The blithe spirit in another --
What else could I ask?

Yet I am asking -- for I need to know that I am a person.

Sounds strange, doesn't it?
After all, when I love them so much,
Why should I want more than being known as "_____'s
    mother"?
I'm proud of each of them.
I'm glad I'm "_____'s mother."

Maybe I just want to be a better mother.
Maybe I want, too, to be able to be M--- at the same time.

But the situation is a mixed-up one --
And I am mixed-up, too.
This has been a bad, bad day!

Help me to be M--- tomorrow.
I love you, Lord.

                                                    Mary Brown

BEING A MOTHER IS

loving one man so completely that you long to be the mother of his child.

going through childbirth with anticipation, patience, and a sense of miracle.

remembering that unique sense of love and oneness with God which husband and wife share at the birth of their child.

holding your newborn for the first time with the assurance that GOD IS.

going home -- to sleepless nights, formula, diapers, routine, responsibility.

letting the house go so you can take time. Time to play and teach pat-a-cake, time to rock and sing, time to hold a sleeping baby, time to grow and become.

being a wife and lover so that your children will know that the love between their parents is special, tolerant, respectful and secure.

teaching a child -- how to say "Da-da", how to wave bye-bye, how to smile, what to touch and what to leave alone. Teaching love, hostility, approval, rejection, friendliness, optimism, pessimism, moodiness through mother-child osmosis.

keeping up -- keeping up with a toddler in the garbage can, with a six-year-old down the street, with new styles; it is staying alert and keeping up with the news so that your child can be proud of you.

assuring your child of your love for her, of her worth, of the security of her home.

a bad day -- when you've yelled at the kids, burned the supper, accomplished nothing and lost your perspective.

asking your child to forgive you when you have been "on her" all day unjustly and loving her when she says she understands.

taking care of a child day in and day out during the pre-school years to the point that you are dependent on her laughter and chatter.

taking your child to school on the very first day with smiles and good wishes while inside you experience the agony of "letting go."

pushing your child into the world and teaching her to be independent while keeping a listening ear and open arms.

helping your child to grow up, and all the while wishing she wouldn't.

Being there -- when there is excitement over a caterpillar, when there is fear over a bad dream, when she falls off a bike, when a disappointment comes, when friends ridicule, when Santa Claus comes.

an honor and an occupation, a frustration and a reward, failure and success, always and just once.

a gift and a calling from God.

Carolyn Henson

A Time to Worship

"O come, let us worship and bow down, let us kneel before the Lord, our Maker."

Psalms 95:6

Worship is the central part of our common life. It is that which we do week after week in order to keep our lives in focus. It is the formal celebration of all of life when the People of God receive their lives as gift and offer their lives as gift. Nothing we do celebrates our wholeness -- limitation and possibility ... grief and gladness ... sin and grace ... fear and faith -- as does worship.

The three prayers which follow were offered during Sunday morning worship services. "Worship" reflects the poverty of our worship. The wealth of worship is reflected in "Discovery" and "Life Is Present." The confession of faith is one person's attempt to articulate his own faith commitment.

A PRAYER

Here we are again -- we're really a motley crew -- thanks for loving us. We rushed from home with the Sunday paper only partly read and we've already yelled at the kids to hurry up so that we could get here fairly close to the starting time for Sunday School. The breakfast was cereal and toast, as usual, and the party last night lasted a little long and we're only part here -- and that part that's here wants to play golf or go home and curl up for another quick nap. Already our stomach is growling and we're tired of sitting. We just sat through a Sunday School class which was less than exciting. Here we are -- we're not much ready to meet with the God of all creation.

These people sitting on our row are really something. A lawyer, an ex-mayor of the city, a big wig at the University, a college professor, a big business tycoon, a football coach, a well-known woman in these parts -- some really sharp people -- I hear we've even got 17 Ph.D.'s in this church -- this is bound to be the zingiest church in town. Oops -- there we go again -- we forgot these people aren't significant because they are important in our eyes; it's because they are just like us all -- human beings and they need to be loved like we do. I think if we saw things like you do we probably would see that what they need is a warm handshake and even perhaps a hug. We all need to know what it is to experience love from a fellow human being and from a person who, like us, is committed to Jesus the Christ.

Remind us that he's not *just* a lawyer or a barber, and she's not *just* a mother, grandmother, or teacher, but that we're all fellow compatriots in life and that a tear shared together as loving friends is more sacred than all of the praise of a detached world. In our need to be loved help us not to forget that our command from you is to love.

Lord, we would like to give our sons and daughters a big hug --
but we seldom do it. We want to put our arm around that
person who has helped us but we just never get around to it. We
want to cry when we're touched by beauty or yourself but we
can't do it before others.

You said that people would be able to pick out a Christ - one in
a crowd because he is a person who loves another. I'm afraid
that isn't the keynote of your church through the world or of
us here today. Well -- we're here -- in a way which is uniquely
and divinely yours, melt the coldness of our hearts, break
through the fences which separate us from you and our
neighbors, and make us sensitive to people -- the people you
died for. Lord here we are. Penetrate into our private world --
Please!! Amen.

Jim Dolby

A PRAYER OF GRATITUDE AND INTERCESSION

Dear God, we come before you today to give thanks and to make intercession.

We give thanks for personal freedom and for those who guard it: For policemen and philosophers; for soldiers and teachers.
For those who lead us, we give thanks and pray wisdom: For Mayor Dudgeon and Governor Smith and President Nixon.

We give thanks that children have parents and that parents have children.
We are grateful for jobs and for salaries.

We give thanks for the past and all its richness, for the present and its vast opportunities, and for the future and its hope.

We make intercession for those who are in anguish over the war -- for all of us, we pray a sense of direction, a clear vision, and charity.
And for the men whose conflict is not just mental, those men who are on the battlefields and in the prison camps, we pray an understanding of Thy Presence, a sense of forgiveness and the strength to hold on.

For the young man whose mind is still asleep, we pray the excitement of discovering truth.
For the one whose world has come unglued this week because of bad news of unexpected bills or the sudden realization that he's getting older, we pray the integrating power of faith and optimism.

For the one who is just plain tired, we pray the courage to leave some things undone so as to regain spirit.
For the woman who is lonely and cut off -- whose personal relationships are limited to simple politeness, we pray the gift of community and friendship.

For the man who is just a bundle of appetites, we pray direction and purpose for living.
For the one who doesn't know who he is, we pray the knowledge that he is the son of God.

Through Christ our Lord, Amen.

Jerry Henson

A PRAYER

Too often, God, we're on the dark side of the cloud -- we can only see ominous grey swirls of mist and rain but on top of that cloud there is light and these same clouds look like vast expanses of pure white cotton. It looks so peaceful and real that we want to climb out of a plane and snuggle up in the billowing miles of inviting softness. That's what happens when light gets onto things, Lord, and most of the time we're without light for our paths.

Most of us here today would like to know what it is to meet with you today -- to see the sun-side of life, but we don't know how to get through the clouds -- we don't have any spiritual jet to do it -- we are left only with shafts of light which help us a little, but these glimpses of light are so infrequent and we forget so easily.

Maybe we really are children of darkness and prefer the dark side so that our pettiness and weaknesses won't show up for what they are. To be really seen like we are would be most painful. Sometimes I think we never grow up but just wander around hoping that things aren't the way they are, and we aren't really bad or self-centered, and that, in the end, Santa Claus really exists, and that the pot of gold is at the end of the rainbow. Then that stream of light illumines our life and we know that this isn't a make-believe world but a cruel, sick, diseased, sinful world -- it has been and always will be. It is a place that needs more light, and we know that the torch has been passed to us. Help us not to drop this torch nor to let it go out through indifference or lack of care.

Even in the darkness we know that we need you and that you can heal when sickness is found and that you will forgive us for not responding to the light we have had. Here we are again, Lord, not just big children but responsible human beings ready to get a glimpse of the sun-side of the cloud -- and to meet with the Son -- The Light of the World. We still prefer darkness, but maybe today we will be able to see you a little better and can see what it means when you instructed us to be a light in an oppressively dark world. Amen.

Jim Dolby

WORSHIP

We come to church on Sunday.

We come with our smug smiles, our pious faces, our Sunday clothes. We come with a mistaken feeling of righteousness, a belief that somehow our presence here pronounces us Christian.

In fact, we come to be seen, and not to see; to meet the right people, not to meet the only man who has ever been truly right; to receive, but not to give. We place our bodies in a chair, but our minds cannot cease their selfish, greedy seeking.

What wonder, then, that we do not worship?

What wonder that we receive nothing from the sermon?

What wonder that we do not go away refreshed?

What wonder that we could not find God -- not even here.

Penny Edens

DISCOVERY

Is that all there is? -- to life-- to love -- to God

A generation that tells it like they think it is -- and few who like the telling!

We found we were wrong about some things we believed --

So we opened our mind on the others -- and at times we were vacant.

Determined that we would not delude ourselves -- with old cliches -- with being so positive

We found something wrong with nearly all that was -- and sought to change -- but to what?

We couldn't let ourselves be sure -- not that sure, for we must always be subject to question --

So we sought a new cause, a new way, or a new thrill, and said -- *this* is living!

But each time we achieved, arrived at our goal, we felt it -- "Is that all there is?" --

Surely there's more -- and yes -- it is so! There's hope that keeps us returning!

There's hope that man, though imperfect, was created for a reason

That we can learn to live -- with being honest -- aware -- with seeking and doing -- and seldom *knowing.*

Hugh McMullen

LIFE IS PRESENT

Learning to live in love
Is escaping from isolation.
Forced by friends, who may be foes,
Encouraged to gain with no evaluation.

Isn't it ignorant or maybe insane,
Saying and sitting and being the same?

Pushed through puberty toward popularity,
Rushed through ruins toward ruthless riches,
Eternally plagued with repeated errors,
Searching for masters in order to serve.
Eventually forgotten but not enlightened
Normal is nothing and nothing is normal
Tragedy is true when truth is not the tyrant.

Bobby Cunningham

A CONFESSION OF FAITH

I believe in God, the one almighty and personal Being, existing without division or inner distinctions, who has created and continues to create and administer the universe according to his own righteous purpose. I believe that in His love and mercy He has extended Himself visibly onto the stage of human history becoming incarnate in the person of Jesus Christ and there adequately demonstrating His nature as redeeming Love for the salvation of a rebellious humanity. I believe that He is, ever has been, and ever will be spiritually present and involved in His universe transforming, guiding, and inspiring those who respond to His saving love, bringing them into true fellowship with Himself and with one another in His Church.

Ron Smith

A Time to Suffer

"If any man would come after me, let him deny himself and take up his cross daily and follow me."

Luke 9:23

We know little of the meaning of suffering with Christ. We have not experienced much of his agony. Yet we live before the mystery of his sacrificial life and death. The glimpse we have had gives us the sense of victory in defeat ... redemption through suffering ... life being born out of death.

Each year on Maundy Thursday or on Good Friday we come together to worship. We gather around tables and celebrate the ritual of communion. We assume the mood of Passion Week and attempt to feel with the Suffering Savior and to anticipate the soon to be celebrated Easter Sunday. In that setting one begins to comprehend the meaning of Good Friday.

The following verse was used as a call to worship for that service. The prayer was written during the Season of Lent in the mood of repentance. "The Tree" points us to the event of God's poured out love in Jesus Christ.

A bald hill

Two beams of wood

Why do we call

This Friday Good?

Deryl Fleming

Lord, I'm trying ...
To pick up my cross, I mean.
It got a little heavy last week
And I dropped it ... or rather, I threw it down
And I cried in self pity ... it's too much.
And I took off the yoke too.
I want out, I said ...
I want to be free.
O, God, what is freedom?
My heart almost broke with the burden of its own freedom.
Lord, today, I want your yoke back.
I set my hand to the plow way back there somewhere ...
Help me, Lord, to quit looking back.
I remember, Lord, it wasn't easy for you either ...
     You cried that day over Jerusalem
     Your friends all said, "Why do you keep on?"
     You stumbled and fell that day on the way to Calvary.
O, Lord, forgive me ...
     For all my whining ...
     For my complaining ...
     For my eternal self pity ...
     For wanting it to be easy ...
Give me your strength so I can carry this cross ...
Give me your grace to carry it even when I don't want to ...
Because I really do love you, Lord ...
Even if I haven't been acting like it lately.

Amen.

Minnie Herring

THE TREE

Teardrops kissed the loam-fields of a tender mother
    And from the bows of death crept life:
        Beginning of an end to begin again.
Leaves lifted by the honey dew, sun-soaked and free
    To surge life-gifted to the heavens.
Bulwark of nature
    Standing strong against the foes of life:
Recorder of history
    Iron-ringed and wise:
        Life giver of man.
Now cut
    Roughhewn and crossed
Oh baneful tree
    Flaw-formed and fierce
Your gnarled and knotted symmetry
    Foretells the murder of all history.
Footstool of God
    And universal stage
Were blood-soaked hands seek for a cleansing tide
    And festered hearts
Beat rancid blood
    To flood the poisoned platform where He died.
His words ring out with every bit ax blow that nicks your base:
"It is finished" -- "It is finished."
    Nailed to your limbs the cry rings loud and long
And soaked into your jagged grain the scenes of death.
    Now, rugged Rood you lie splintered, split, and done!

Gary Don Boyd

A Time to Die

"None of us lives to himself, and none of us dies to himself. If we live, we live to the Lord, and if we die, we die to the Lord; so then, whether we live or whether we die, we are the Lord's."

Romans 14:7-8

Death, too, is a part of life. So we celebrate it. Not with the ease and eagerness with which we celebrate much of life, but with the confidence that life is stronger than death ... with the sadness that comes with separation from our "dearly beloved."

Ours is a young community. We have not often been brought up against death. But when we have experienced it we have known to "ask not for whom the bell tolls, the bell tolls for thee."

A deeply loved member of the fellowship wrote "The Gate Keeper" as she lived with death in those last days. "Death and Life" was written during the week following the death of a father-in-law. "Death," written by one of our children, presents a child's feelings about the grim reality. "Heaven's Fashion Show" and "The Good Life" point respectively to the demand and the gift that death calls forth.

THE GATE KEEPER

Death, I have glimpsed your shadow many times;
Now it looms larger, nearer; but no fear
Have I, for you are keeper of the gate
That opens to my Father's house. Not here,
But only at your gate is entrance found;
And none but you can open it for me,
For you alone, dear Death, possess the key.

How could I dread your coming? For I know --
I have assurance from my Father's word --
That greater joy than Earth can give or show
Awaits me: "Eye hath seen not, nor ear heard,
Neither hath entered into heart of man
The things God hath prepared" -- prepared for me!
How could I, then, aught else than happy be?

I wait with patience, Death, till you shall come
To firmly and yet gently take my hand.
Whether you lead up rugged hills of pain
Or through the peaceful dark, at your command
I shall walk with you unafraid. I know
That you will open wide for me the gate
Where love and joy unspeakable await.

                              Stella Osgood Humphrey

DEATH AND LIFE

What do you write when you have been told to write?

Perhaps there is nothing to write about ... or maybe too much.

Or maybe it's just that you can't get it into words that say what you feel.

But then to say it is more important than the words you use ... I guess.

This week it would almost certainly have to be about death

Because death is what this week is full of.

It's strange though, because in the most real way I know this death is completely overshadowed by life.

Life, capitalized ... life that shines ... life that moves.

Life that reaches out to people ... especially old people ... especially young people.

Life that meets no strangers ... or at least changes strangers into friends ... enduring friends.

Life that in its essence reaches out to God ... through His Son ... to His children ... to me.

Life as it is meant to be and for which there is no death

Jan Williams

DEATH

Death sounds scarey. It sounds like murder, suffocation and disease. Yet God says it is something to look forward to. Negroes used to give a big party when someone died. They lived such an unhappy life that death sounded good. But it still scares me. Sometimes I feel like death isn't really anything, just make-believe. I guess that's because no one really close to me has died. One relative died around a year ago. But I didn't really know her that well. The only difference now is when we go see our grandparents we have one less relative to visit. God seems to say death is happiness. Sort of like on those scary shows where the girl is alone in the old mansion. Suddenly she hears a noise and goes to see what it is. She comes to a door and starts to open it. With God the door represents death. And on the other side is a sunny, happy meadow. Jesus told his disciples there would be riches there because that is what would make them happy. I'd like to be with my friends and family, so I think I'll find that there. At school there's a girl from a children's home. She said that her sister hated her and a lady there wished she'd go blind. She tried in minor ways to kill herself today. I don't know if she was kidding or really meant it. Now that I'm writing this I feel a little better about death.

Susan Brister

HEAVEN'S FASHION SHOW

They had a fashion show in Heaven
For all folk and their kin.
But some of the richly dressed people
Were the ones that couldn't get in.
They didn't model the Paris fashion,
Or the latest evening gown.
The garments they had for all to see
Were a great deal more profound.

The shoes were made of peace and goodwill,
They had a permanent shine.
Their clothes were made of pale righteousness,
The lining was quite divine.
Their belt was sown from untarnished truth,
A lie could never slip out.
Their hat was the gift of salvation from God,
The slight trimming was devout.
Their handbag contained the word of God --
They'd carry it all their life.
To top it they had faith as their coat,
To help them through times of strife.
The things they wore would never wear out,
They'd pass each years' fashion test.
And by using perpetual prayer
They'd all stay their Sunday best.

I wondered as I stood there in line,
Waiting my ticket to buy,
If when I finally reached the front
My purse would be a bit shy.
For 'though I had plenty of money,
I could look over and see
Folks on the other side of the gate
Were truly richer than me.

Charlotte Carpenter

THE GOOD LIFE

Life is a watermelon feast.

And I'm gonna pick the ripest, plumpest one in the patch, and put it in the stream to cool.

And while it's coolin' I'm gonna build me a shelter from the sun, right over there where I can watch the waters run by, and look into the distance and see the mountains still white with snow, and the trees fresh green, and wonder at the beauty of the earth.

And when that watermelon's good and cold, I'm gonna bust it open and grab me a handful of the heart. And the cold, sweet juice will run down my front, and I'll put my hand in again and again, 'til I've eaten so much my insides feel cool too. Then I'll wash off the sticky juice in the stream, and rest me a while.

Then when I'm all rested and feeling right with the world, I'm gonna get a bucket of water and clean off that shelter I built. Then I'm gonna take some of the seed and plant them over there in the sun, because that melon was so fine.

And when I get to heaven, I'm gonna look down and watch someone find my shelter in glad surprise, and go to the patch and pick one of those melons that grows from the seed I planted. And he's gonna build a table while his melon's cooling.

And I'm gonna sit and reflect on the goodness of life.

Amen.

Penny Edens

A Time to be Reborn

"If Christ has not been raised, your faith is futile and you are still in your sins."

I Corinthians 15:17

Easter is a glad time for the Community of Faith. It is one of two pivotal events in our existence, the other being the Festival of the Incarnation (Advent and Christmas). More than any other season, Easter defines the mission and hope of the church.

The first two poems were written as theme interpretations for Sunday morning worship. Printed on the worship bulletin, they set the mood for the celebrations of Easter Sunday and the Sunday after Easter. "Empty Cross" was written to reflect the mood of victory.

To hear the beat of a different drummer
     To dance to the rhythm of a different tune
          To go with the sound of a different track
                         that is the quest

To shuck the same old nothingness
     To be done with the same old mediocrity
          To be free of the same old hang-ups
                         that is the quest

It's an Easter quest
               Nothing less than new creation
               Only death and resurrection

Turning a new leaf
                    Praying a new prayer
                              Wearing a new suit
                    won't do it
Only a miracle
                    can do it
                              Miracle of miracles
               God above the gods
Life in the midst of death

Easter is come
               not come and gone
                         but come to stay
                              today

Easter belongs to the now generation
     This is the day of new creation
God is God of the living
     Life is given to the seeking

This is the quest
          to follow the Christ
                    Those who do
                         know the new
They are the new creation
               God's Easter People.

Deryl Fleming

To stop and stay here satisfied with these ways
    to live in the past and feed on the old days
        (not as good as they now seem
            not as bad as they might have been)
To sew up and hem in
    to nail down and close out

People in their places
        and things as they are (or used to be)
    is the urge of the human
        the cry of the man and the woman

But God says no
    to the status quo
    Greater works than these shall you do
    Behold I make all things new

He lets loose life and commands the living
    He calls for a new present and ushers in a new future
    He scatters the cliques and reconciles the enemies
    He releases the captive and sets the prisoner free

Man says no
    it's too much to bear, too hard to endure
    if we can't be sure, everything's insecure
        And besides

    we like it the way it is
    we want it the way it was

No, says God
    and some men see
        God's no is his yes

Yes to life and love
    yes to truth and persons
        yes to one and all

And some say Amen ... so be it ... Yes, Lord
    They are his Easter People
    He is their God, the God of the living

    Deryl Fleming

EMPTY CROSS

A cross points straight up
    to show its destiny and
    object of devotion.

A cross reaches out on
    both sides to show
    its encompassing
    concern.

A cross sinks low
    to show the humility
    and surrender of the
    One who made it live

A silent, empty cross speaks
    loudly of resurrection
    power.

Donna McMullen

A Time of Transition

"When I was a child, I spoke like a child, I thought like a child, I reasoned like a child; when I became a man, I gave up childish ways."

I Corinthians 13:11

The developmental process of persons in the church is a pilgrimage of faith. It is a continual growing up into Christ. The transition from one era to another is an occasion for deep religious experience as well as a situational change. The significant events in a Christian's life are also full of religious significance.

Graduation is a signal event in the lives of many of us and thus in the "life together" that is the church. It marks a new era in the educational and vocational pilgrimage, and thus in the life of faith. At the commencement service of Richfield High School one of our fellowship offered the "Prayer for Graduation."

"Tribute to a Daughter-In-Law" and "The Golden Years" reflect the simple and profound meanings of the time when the children marry and leave home to establish a new home. "I Saw Her" follows one through the stages on life's road. "The Lost Secrets" remind us of the urgency of life.

PRAYER FOR GRADUATION

Dear Lord,

Here we are!

-- the stubborn, selfish, sickening, careless, carefree, overly-ambitious, complacent people that we are, and we hurt. We hurt because war doesn't bother us; hunger doesn't bother us; sickness, crime, and violence don't bother us.

We just don't care anymore.

We're filthy, O God, and it's hard for us to believe that You love us even if we are filthy -- but I guess that's because we've forgotten what love means, too.

Give us the power, Lord, to live out our full potential -- to say or do something that's good in this ol' world.

We're together tonight for the last time -- give us the courage to make this night a new beginning rather than the end of something exciting. We are terribly finite and inconstant creatures, but we can create something lasting if we recognize life as the gift that it is and live it one day at a time.

It's been a good day.

Thank you for this moment.

Amen.

Buzz Brown

TRIBUTE TO A DAUGHTER-IN-LAW

I look at that stoop-shouldered, bearded young clod,
Supposedly made in the image of God,
Rememb'ring his foolish mistakes as a kid,
The stupid and ludicrous things that he did,
Searching in wonder this boy grown to man
To find the perfection she sees, if I can.
But she in her wife-love is totally blind
To faults that my mother-love yet seem to find.

I suddenly gain new respect for his life,
For he had the wisdom to find him a wife
Who loves him completely, adores him as is,
Is ready to love anything that is his.
I see he is stronger, more thoughtful and wise,
Becoming the man that he sees in her eyes.
I have to admit I can't figure it yet --
But Lord, just how lucky can one mother get!

Penny Edens

THE GOLDEN YEARS

Horray, hurrah, it's really great,
My teen-age kids are grown and gone.
At last we can afford a steak
And pay a man to mow the lawn.

The telephone no longer rings,
The tub is mine alone. I find
That every dawn a new day brings
Of quiet peace, and easy mind.

So what's the reason that I sit
With all the peace I craved at last
And have a stupid crying fit,
And turn the Hi-Fi on full blast?

Penny Edens

I SAW HER

I saw her dancing in a moonlit field without a care.
I saw the innocence of a blush upon her cheek,
A ribbon wound neatly in her hair.
    And I saw her as a child.

I saw her standing beneath the chandeliers of time.
I watched the rosebud blossom in her cheeks;
And saw her eyes sparkling like diamonds in a velvet sky.
    I saw her as a lady.

I saw her crying in the stillness of a night
Dewdrops on lovely-petaled leaves, softly sobbing.
A tender rose, her petals pale from thoughts of loved ones lost.
    I saw her as a woman.

I saw her kissing infant tears aside:
Caressing, as a gentle breeze might seeth a fragile flower's leaf
Watched her love a babe.
    I saw her as a mother.

I saw her as a rosebud--now blossoming--now blushing--now dying.
And I shall say I knew her, and I loved her.
And the echoes of my mind repeat-repeat-repeat
    I saw her.

Gary Don Boyd

THE LOST SECRETS

I found an ancient parchment once.
Excitement grew; I read the page.
The inscriptions strange; but, soon I know,
Were teachings of a long lost sage.

He found his solace much too late;
A lonely life had been the cost.
He found the weak are those who hide
From truth; his happiness was lost.

He knew that all of us play roles;
Some with false pride; some with fear.
I wish that all had read his words.
He ended with these statements here:

"Grasp the truth within your life.
Search the workings of the heart.
Open and reveal yourself;
And let another's love take part!"

Bob Wayne Ousley

A Time to be Surprised

"And he who sat upon the throne said, 'Behold, I make all things new.'"

Revelation 21:5

We have learned to expect a sense of "newness" at certain times of the year. We have also learned that we are often surprised by God. In quiet places and in noisy rooms, in sacred literature and in secular voices, in great crises and in simple meetings, in rude awakenings and in rituals of friendship, we are met by God.

The following selections recall some of the surprises experienced by the Church.

THE SHOWER

My teardrops fell like sadness with the rain
And yet my heart could smile and bear no shame;
The fear that's spawned from needing such success
By failure, has the right to cause distress.
A constant hope that sunshine will appear
Requires a prayer and strength to cast out fear.
The whys of damaged pride and cause of tears
Are cleansed with prayers for happy distant years.
My tears are for the weak who shrink from pain
And realize not that flowers follow rain.

                                    Bob Wayne Ousley

BETWEEN

I looked into the sun and saw the moon.
I wept when others laughed.
I felt the frost amongst the flames of life.
I found I was a fool.

I was sleeping with despair.
I was kissed by every darkness.
I was scared to say farewell.
I stepped into the sun, and smiled.

                                    Bob Wayne Ousley

THE WAY OF JESUS

The ethic of Jesus is inseparable from the remainder of the gospel he lived and proclaimed. It is an integral and essential part of his understanding of man's relation to God. The commitment of faith is prerequisite. One must be a citizen of the Kingdom in order to live the life of the Kingdom.

Obedience may be described as full response to the demand of love, the kind of love shown in Jesus himself. The ethic is not, therefore, one of adherance to rules or of conformity to external norms, but of being the Christ-like person and doing the Christ-like things in the various episodes of moral existence. The very nature of that existence requires such an approach.

It is only in each situation that informed by the gospel witness, alive to the indwelling Christ, and sensitive to the reality of the present, the clear demand of the love of Jesus comes to the responsive disciple. The call is to *be* a responsive disciple.

An ethic based on these foundations means that one can neither fall back on a legalism, nor be content with a mere mechanical imitation of Jesus. It means that he must be not only receptive but creative, not only informed, but in tune. It means that he must be ready to act faithfully and courageously, undertaking a new moral adventure at each point of decision. To face life in this way is not easy. It is, in fact, somewhat frightening. It is also, however, the way of responsibility, and, more than this, the way of Jesus.

Ron Smith

A PRAYER FOR THE 20TH CENTURY READER

O God,
Give me books to read and thoughts to think to take me beyond where I am. May I read:

Thoreau
       above the noise of TV, stereo, and kids
the newspaper and the letters of Paul
       with equal urgency
Drs. Spock, Gesell, and Ginott
       and still have courage to make up my own mind
both Time and U.S. News and World Report
       with an open mind
Mr. Rabbit's Dinner Party
       with enthusiasm
the lyrics of the Beatles
       and wake up singing
Tennessee Williams
       to acknowledge my own sinfulness
Freud
       without becoming a pessimist
James Baldwin
       through the black man's eyes
Dostoevsky
       to participate in the guilt of all men

O God,
All truth is yours. May I listen to the world.

Amen.

Beverly Fleming

THE LORD IS MY COACH

The Lord is my coach,

With Him on my side

Never can I be defeated

Or have reason to hide.

The Lord is my coach,

He calls each play

That I make

Day by day.

The Lord is my coach,

And a good one, too.

If you didn't know,

He also will help you.

Bart Jenkins

THE TRIUMPH

The most dangerous endeavor is to be a friend.

The most exciting part of this is growth, unity, understanding and mutual maturation.

The most rewarding feeling is to give a hand, an encouragement, a needed shoulder, or a thing or two, and not o'erstep "The Boundaries".

The most depressing occurrence is to cross "The Boundary" and struggle with petty jealousy.

The most Godlike emotion results in the clasping of a friend, and then rejoicing in forgiveness.

Bob Wayne Ousley

If the heavens declare the glory
        of God,
Then I know a wonderful thing --
There are millions and millions of
        people around
Whose being declares the same thing!

Donna McMullen

My eyes wink and blink;
My nose twitches and itches;
This leads me to think that people
        who run and jump and crawl
                and sit and walk
        are wonderful,
                wonderful items of Creation

Donna McMullen

Trembling,
> I knocked once more
>> And hoped no one was home.
>>> Sickened by the squallor,
> Appalled at the unsightly shambles
>>> Called by some folks, "flats", I stood.

Cowering,
> She pushed the door ajar
>> And gaped into my eyes.
>>> "The church ... the church in town
> Wants you to have these clothes. We ... we thought
>>> You'd like to have some groceries too."

Shuddering,
> I handed her the simple gift
>> And turned to leave.
> "Thank you," she said, "I knew He would provide."

Restlessly,
> I trudged through the mud up the long
>> Dirt road back to my car.
>>> The cries of sick and frightened babies
> And the sights of laughless children haunted me on my
>>> Journey back to where I had been before I came
>>> To this side of life.

Anxiously,
> I had given Mrs. No-one not much of
>> Something that I had.
>>> To her it meant another week's existence
> In the squalid land of fear and dread. To her it was
>>> A lot, for she had taught herself not to expect
>>> At all.

Fearfully,
> She had given more than all she had.
>> From her unlovely lips, from those unsightly shacks
>>> Called slums, within a
> Barren and a horrid place her voice had threatened me.
>>> It was the voice of God!

Gary Don Boyd

HOW LONG DOES A FRIEND REMAIN?

I whispered to my friend (who was not here), "How are you?"
I cried into my pillow (wet with something), "Please stay with
     me."
I felt that all the things around me meant so little;
All I needed for a cheerful day was one hand to say, "Hello" ...
It never came.
The days have fallen from the wall, the nights still hang on
     clotheslines.
An occasional greeting has met the social need,
But not the love ...
Oh, how to learn that expectation is so futile, and must be met
     with stones.
Only fools plan to love and then be loved ... liked?
Well ...
Sadness costs so little and strength is priced so high,
But friends are romantic fantasies that live in dreams and
     dime-store literature.
Why dreams? Because of tests and modern daily chores a friend
     is one who loves.
If you're there to entertain,
If his time allows a moment.
So brace yourself for isolation, for living in a shell, my
     "friend"!
A friend remains as long as he
Can use your love, and still be free.

Bob Wayne Ousley

PASTOR

The Man of Silence comes when I know sorrow,
But no word he says --
No black-creped hand he offers,
But rather shows me by the way he comes
That he has sorrowed, too.
He and Christ, they understand.
And suddenly my wall of stone gives 'way before that indrawn
wind of caring
And I can cry.

The Man of Silence comes when I am ill.
He offers no trite platitude,
No sugar pill of pious prayer,
But with a look, a word, recalls
That all must suffer, all must die
Even Christ and he,
And by his look the magnitude of my own torment fades away
And I accept with thanks my suffering.

The Man of Silence stands before me in my pulpit.
This time he speaks, but still
There are no wasted words, no hackneyed phrase,
But in their place a deep and measured truth,
A word to answer me my present need,
And from that silent vessel I am filled,
And marvel once again that to this place and people,
Christ has sent The Man of Silence.

In Grateful Appreciation,
The Body that is the People of Lake Shore

A PRAYER

Dear Lord, ----- there, we did it again. We started to pray and called you Lord, and we're not sure what it means, and we know it's not much of a reality in our lives.

If it means that we should accept our lives as a gift from you, we feebly give thanks -- but most of the time we believe and act like we're in control of our lives. We have protected ourselves from every angle -- we have car, hospital, house, liability and life insurance -- the latter one just in case our "luck" runs out. We own guns to protect us from intruders, have special locks on the door, put our money in good banks. We pay taxes for policemen and firemen to protect us, and we know about our great army, navy, and air force who protect us nationally. We systematically have our car checked out to make sure its safe -- the tires are good, the brakes work well, and on top of it all it's mighty nice looking. We can sure take care of things ourselves -- except for those rare experiences -- the time when we almost hit the other car head on, or the time we looked at the face of a friend or a loved one in a coffin -- we wonder when our clock will tick the last time -- then we are reminded that you are the giver and sustainer of life. Thanks for this reminder.

If calling you Lord means that we ask you often what is your will or pleasure for us we aren't much at that either. Most of us are middle class, white, Americans -- and our job is pretty well set out for us -- we must work hard to make money, get some security, and have some fun -- occasionally we tip you for keeping things quiet and pleasant, and for being our guardian angel.

To ask you what to do with our life, our time, our money, our marriage, our reading, our leisure, our abilities -- that's old fashioned -- after all the old saying "what was good for Paul and Silas is good enough for me", is just part of a hackneyed song -- it's not mod. But we often feel so lonely and we don't want to be alone, and we feel anxious and guilty so often -- maybe there is a dimension to life which we've thrown out in our 20th century, scientific society -- maybe a man can have communion with you and can know what is right for him and perhaps there may be some truth in that Paul and Silas song.

We're so proud -- can't we see in the birth of a child, or in a beautiful budding rose, or in the fresh breezes of spring, or in the dimensions of space your care and involvement with us? So often it takes the cold hand of death or the heat of sickness to realize that we're living on given time and that almost everything we do is vanity.

What we're saying is that we really don't know what it means to call you Lord -- the giver of our lives and one who wants to be our *friend* and *king*. Just now in our middle-class way -- just now we want to start praying all over again -- Lord -----. Amen.

Jim Dolby

PROBING

The lights faintly flickering form starlite symbols in the night
Which guide me over the rough-grounded field
And through the grasping, pulling sea of grasses which cling to
  me.

I stumble, fall, arise and stumble in a never-ceasing cycle,
Trying, but never achieving perfect stability
In this darkened, star-studded, rough-grounded, weed-covered
  field.

"Press on, endure and meet the tasks of life!"
This inner voice of mine has persuasive power
Probing me to probe the possibilities of life.

If I do not examine all I can in life,
Then truly I shall be blinded by the darkness,
And in utter darkness fall and remain fallen,
Over-grown with the tangly, grasping grasses of the field.

If I probe life to the fullest, perhaps I shall discover that
In this rough-grounded field covered with grass and weeds
There is a path leading to an adventure which fulfills my total
  being.

To probe life to the fullest and find the possibilities,
Or to fear finding is the overwhelming choice I face.
And all the while the sacred scripture rings throughout eternity:
"Few there be that find."

Gary Don Boyd

Occasionally the word gets out
    it may keep for decades or centuries
        guarded carefully by the keepers of such secrets
but somehow it slips
        through a crack or over a wall
and all the world hears
        that God is dead
    or at best
        asleep

In our time man has left Him behind
    too tired for our trip
        too worn for our ways
a God that can't keep up with man
        will not do
    So we leave Him
        behind
        in the old-fashioned and outmoded
    and we go on with life
        on our own

Free from God
    we romp and stomp
        roar and soar
until in the road ahead
        around a bend
    we find Him again
        not dead but alive
        not asleep but awake
        not behind us but before us

What we left behind
        was not God
        but our image of God, our ideas about God.

        Deryl Fleming

Father in heaven,
You do not act as we expect
the Lord of Lords to act.
You "miss the chance"
to do the obvious
that would proclaim your worth.
The things you do are so simple
and unsung
that we who are prepared for
	commercials, big campaigns and slogans,
will be forced to "rate" you low.
There's a nagging thought, however.
Is God a "sleeper"?
Will God finish strong?

Donna McMullen

A Time to Re-create

"Be still and know that I am God ..."

Psalms 46:10

Summer brings sun and fun, recreation and re-creation for the People of God. It is, indeed, the opportunity to be whole ... to refresh body and renew spirit ... to be with nature ... to talk to the animals ... to search for soul ... to explore and explode ... to be astounded by the wonders of the world around us.

It is a time for reflection for some, particularly the young. The following poems and the short story came out of the creative reservoir of teenagers of the community and the summer sun and shade.

THE IMPOSSIBLE SILENCE

Sometimes the human should be alone, I say,

Let him take the time to think or pray.

Let him just lie there without a noise --

And he may find a meaningful joy.

Of course there is always a telephone or a plane overhead,

Or your stomach saying, "I want to be fed."

If you're outside, someone will be mowing;

Or you're in a room by yourself, with the air-conditioner
going.

Is silence impossible? I'm afraid so ...

Unless you were dead, when your heartbeat wouldn't go.

So, maybe a person should listen all around,

For that cry of help when another's down.

And give what is needed for a silent sound,

And listen for love with that God you have found.

Vicki Martin

I WONDER

I've been told a hundred times,
The way my life should be.
I've been shown a hundred times,
The things that I should see.

I've said a thousand times,
The way I'd like to live.
I've seen a thousand times,
Things I wish that I could give.

I have wondered a million times,
The way I really am.
And I have wondered a million times,
If I should give a damn.

One will live for the future,
Another one for the past.
I call the first one - Dreamer,
And Reminiscers are the last.

I try to live for today.
And mix life's tasks with my fun.
But usually the fun takes the day,
And I'm wishing the job was done.

But who tells you the way to live,
And who knows which way to go?
There is an answer God could give.
Would I accept Him, though?

Daryl Barrett

TOMORROW

Tomorrow is -- uncertain and very unorganized
            something to look forward to
            something to plan for in detail
            my future
            to find out if my dreams will really come true
            never final because there's always another
                tomorrow
            will it bring peace or destruction?

Julie Spain

ANN

When I met Ann, we were in the sixth grade. She was lonely, afraid, and a complete outcast. I didn't associate with her then. In fact, it wasn't until ninth grade when I saw her again. She had changed quite a bit. Seemed happier and had some friends -- from the Children's Home.

Ann was in my first three classes and I really got to know her. She began to talk to me and it was then I realized that she needed a real friend -- someone to talk to. I found out she was a girl with problems, and I knew all of them.

Before too long I learned the history of her life. Ann was born in a big city. As she grew up, she realized she wasn't as rich as some, and the painful beatings she received were torture. Every evening, her beatings would get harder and harder. Yet, in spite of this, she still loved her mother.

Her grandmother, who lived across town, was the only person who was sweet to her. One evening when Ann went to visit her with her brothers, her mother, and her father, they had a wreck. When Ann woke up, she saw a lady dressed in white and a strange room. Something like she had never seen before. With her body covered with bandages and plaster, she turned and looked at her mother. She, too, was wrapped in bandages. One look at her mother and she burst into tears.

Soon the nurse came and Ann asked to see her brothers and her father. She was told that she could see her brothers in a few days, but she would never see her father again. He was dead.

Ann began to grow and their money began to shrink. Before too long, she was sent to the Children's Home to live.

Ann is still at the Home. Her mother visits her about once a month and she looks forward to every one of them.

This story isn't finished yet because her life isn't. In a way, it just began.

Darla Barrett

A Time to Move

"By faith Abraham . . . went out not knowing where he was to go."

Hebrew 11:8

Summer also brings change. It uproots and transplants the tender children of God. It moves them from one community to another -- to new jobs . . . new schools . . . new houses. By the time they leave us they belong to us and are a part of us. We've learned to rejoice with one another and weep with one another. To see some of our own move on brings sad excitement to the community. We send them on their way to new occasions, glad for them and sad for ourselves.

"On Departing" was written to focus the meaning of change in the light of faith and used as a theme interpretation for a morning worship service in late May. A copy is sent to departing families as a momento of their days in the church and of their move to another city.

Ours is a transient community composed of young families on the move. While we have a significant number of families who have been in the church from the beginning, a large part of the congregation has always been "new" to us. They come and stay a few years (sometimes a few months) and then move with their jobs to a new place. "Come and Gone" reflects our feelings about so many dear persons and families that once belonged to us and now live in other places and with us belong to a fellowship that spans miles and ages.

ON DEPARTING

The God who calls men into being and into New Being
    Who is in every meeting of person with person
        The Mystery behind the mysteries

Now calls men of faith
    to give thanks for the gift of life
              and the mystery of life shared
    to repent of the failure to give oneself
              and the refusal to receive the other
    to turn and receive the Good News of Jesus Christ
              that to men of faith
        The past is utterly forgiven
        The present is utterly given
        The future is utterly open

He calls men to leave
        lands and homes and fathers
    to go out not knowing where
        to look for that City "not made with hands"
    to leave the old securities
        and seize the new and creative insecurity

He calls men to go
        not back home, but into a new wide open
    to forsake
      that they may find
          to depart
            that they may embrace

To his Easter People he promises
    not the "old smooth prizes," but the "new rough prizes"
      'Behold, I make all things new'
            and his presence
      'Lo, I am with you always'
nothing else,
      only newness and presence

And that is enough
there is nothing else
only new beginning and new community
for to live is to
receive life as gift
and give life as love
To the Man of Faith
every death is a resurrection
every ending a beginning
So let us go on
and remember who we are
and Whose we are

Deryl Fleming

COME AND GONE

Suddenly they came
Like a stranger in the night
And plunged themselves
Into our community
Then a year or two
Three or four
They pack up
And open a new door
Gone as quickly
As they came

Never would one have guessed
They would mean so much
Be so dear
Give so freely
But they came
And they came back
They gave
And they kept giving
Soon they had a place in our heart
And gave to us a place in the sun

Now they move on
But not as they came
For they have marked
And been marked by
The gift of community
From far away
They will love and give
Notes and cards, prayers and thoughts
All re-present to us
Their Being

We shall not forget
Nor shall we get over
Their love
Their laughter
Their lives

Deryl Fleming

A Time to Wait

"They who wait for the Lord shall renew their strength, they shall mount up with wings as eagles, they shall run and not be weary, they shall walk and not faint."

Isaiah 40:31

The soul has its seasons too. The season of waiting can come at any time and it comes often. It is a painful time for active, aggressive people like us. But it's a necessary time, an occasion of learning -- of God, of life, or ourselves. Waiting is not passive, we have learned. It is the active seeking of God's presence and power.

Some deliberate times of waiting have become very special to us. Two such occasions are retreats and the communion service. The two selections which follow reflect something of what the church has discovered as it "waits" for the Lord.

Each of us has his own time and way of "waiting." Such times are shared in "Discovery" and "The Quiet Places."

RETREAT

It's 24 fighting Baylor Bears and 1 Aggie
It's the rat who comes to get away from the maze and the
    human who returns to run his course
It's too little sleep and too much fried chicken
It's giving away your pennies and receiving love
It's laughing with one another and crying at the beauty of life
It's being afraid to reveal yourself and finding that others have
    similar feelings
It's loud music and quiet thoughts
It's sharing another's life and discovering yourself
It's having a flat tire and a full spirit
It's Butterfield 8 and breakfast at 9
It's tearing down useless walls of estrangement and building a
    web of relationships
It's listening closely and talking loudly
It's fellowship and solitude
It's digging through the trash and sorting out your soul
It's rose colored glasses and a real look at yourself
It's being given thirty minutes with a stranger and discovering a
    brother
It's love and joy
It's freedom and participation
It's intense and meaningful
It's life
It's good
It's ours

Kathy Kolar

COMMUNION

Bread and Wine give life
        and symbolize Life
classic symbols of mankind
        they represent
    body and soul, substance and spirit
        the totality of human existence
for 2000 years of Christian history they have represented
        Life and Death
    The death of Christ that we might live
        the life of Christ that we might die (in dying we live)

The table is the familiar gathering place
        of people in all places and ages
it's design is not for mere eating
        but for eating together
    for sharing food and personhood
whenever persons gather round a table
    and truly break bread together
        communion happens
    The Lord's table is any table
    surrounded by his people
Those who choose to belong to him and all his children

Come to the table
        let us break bread together
    let us drink wine together
    let us praise God together

Let us celebrate the past to awaken the future
    let us participate in remembrance that we may take on hope.

        Deryl Fleming

DISCOVERY

I searched here and there as I stumbled life's road, for I wanted
a talent to give to my Lord.
I wept many tears, for my talents were few; but my Lord said
"Weep not! I want only you."

"You don't need a talent", my Lord to me sighed. "You just
need a will that is blended with mine.
You needn't shine out as the world's brightest star. You just
need to bring your heart; come as you are!"

So I stopped all my weeping and fumbling about, and I opened
my heart and finally cried out.
And as my song soared, a talent was born -- a talent to dedicate
just to my Lord!

Beverly Hill

THE QUIET PLACES

My Lord comes to me in the quiet places,
The quiet places in my life.
I feel my heart leaping up to him in gladness;
Suddenly there's beauty everywhere.
There is no room for grief and sadness;
His love and goodness fill the air.

My Lord comes to me in the quiet places,
The quiet places in my life.
These golden moments prepare me for tomorrow;
On his strength my hungry soul does feed;
Then in the time of stress and sorrow
I find the faith and strength I need.

Thank you, my Lord, for the quiet places
In my life.

Penny Edens

A Time to Begin Again

"Restore to me the joy of thy salvation."

Psalms 51:12

The Fall is a season of renewal. In our society September is more of a new beginning than January. For the church, too, Autumn is a time of dedication -- a time when we have new energy and enthusiasm to offer to God. So we "start over" with new educational programs, a new stewardship campaign, election of new deacons, and other events of newness.

The following selections are celebrations of two of these events. The first is a light hearted "sounding forth" -- as are many of our celebrations -- written during a budget campaign. The second is a prayer offered in a deacon ordination service.

ODE TO BUDGET PLEDGERS

How about them budget pledgers,
  Ain't they loves?
Pledging that money,
  Helping them doves.
How about them budget pledgers,
  Ain't they right on the dot?
Pledging that money,
  Hot toppin' that parking lot.
Oh, them groovy budget pledgers,
  Ain't they a boon?
Pledging that money,
  Helping Lottie Moon.
Them budget pledgers,
  They has got to be the most.
Paying some of them notes,
  Letting others coast.
Pledging them dollars right on cue,
  Buying them books for B.Y.P.U.
Helping them Baylors,
  Reaching out they hand,
Helping them missions,
  All over the land.
Repairing that parsonage,
  Making it neat.
Keeping that preacher,
  Off of the street.
How to be a budget pledger?
  They ain't nothing to it.
Just pick up a budget card,
  And then just do it!

George Williams

A PRAYER FOR DEACONS

God of Creation,
    God of Life,
God of Grace,
    and God of Glory,
On this fellowship of Deacons pour Thy power.

We do not come to this occasion as men "worthy" of the distinction -- Deacon;
For the distinction of Deacon is not one of worthiness nor attainment, O Lord,
But rather commitment of life, direction, and purpose
In service and ministry through the church of our Lord and Saviour, Jesus Christ.
The ordination of Deacons does not carry with it any magic or mystical power;
For following this very meaningful experience, we shall still be sinful men,
Saved only by the Grace of our ever-living, ever-forgiving, and ever-loving Lord.

The ordination service *does* say that as Christian men we are willing to live the responsible, committed, disciplined life expected of the spiritual leaders of this congregation and the Kingdom of God.

This is our prayer for Ken and Byron, our Father, as they begin their pilgrimage in this new and challenging dimension of their life. May their lives -- and the lives of all of us who bear the name "Deacon" -- truly be the *Salt* of the earth, the *Light* of the world, heirs of the *Keys of the Kingdom,* provided only through the redeeming grace of the Christ in whose name we pray. Amen.

Alton Pearson

A Time to Give Thanks

"It is good to give thanks to the Lord ..."

Psalm 92:1

Historically not one of the holy seasons, yet Thanksgiving is that for the People of God. For they celebrate the sacred in and through the secular. Thanksgiving is not only the occasion of turkey and the trimmings and the big game between Texas and A&M, but also a time for worship ... a time to give thanks to God in the presence of his people.

It has become a high time in the life of our community. On Wednesday evening before Thanksgiving Day we come together to rejoice in and be glad for the goodness of life. We begin with worship and conclude with an informal time of fellowship.

The first two expressions of gratitude were offerings presented by individuals and designed to lead the whole congregation in worship. They focused on the family and the nation. The third selection is two prayers written and offered at mealtime by one of the residents of the home for retired teachers.

WHAT IS A FAMILY?

It is a hug around the neck and a gentle kiss when I come home.

It is a hand-made clay ash tray and a tie from my children on my birthday.

It is a person who listens and tries to understand when I verbally unweave my hopes and fears.

It is the soft touch of a friend who cares.

It is a mother who worries when a child is sick.

It is a father who gets angry when frustrated and it is also a father who cares so much for his family he would do anything for them.

It is a whispered "I love you" from the children.

It is spilled milk, dropped spoons, and a laugh at a child's view of life.

It is Polly, Molly, Shadow, and a picture drawn in school.

It is ballet, piano, and art lessons.

It is a fireplace and a soft chair.

It is a set of responsibilities and careful concern.

It is a spanking and a hug good night.

It is frayed tempers and an understanding smile.

It is a skinned knee and a bandaid.

It is warmth on a cold night.

It is bills and receipts and things.

It is Bluebirds, Campfire Girls; as a matter of fact, it is all girls.

It is chicken a la king and hamburger.

It is a place of decision and hope for the future.

It is a prayer that goes "We thank you for mommy and daddy and this food," Amen.

It is a home-made dress, a picture, and a proud "well done."

It is the Beetles and the Nutcracker Suite.

It is brown and blond hair, blue eyes, eyes that will see the joy and the despair of the realities around us.

It is champaigne and Koolaid.

It is light in a dark world.

It is people who love and who are loved in return.

It is a Christmas visit and a proud parent.

It is reality and fantasy.

It is God's gift to me.

It is a fight and a helping hand.

It is hot and cold water in the shower.

It is a place for tears and a place for laughter.

It is a house, a car, and a new tree.

It is school, work, and never ending responsibility.

It is a calm stillness and a thundering storm.

It is fear for the future and hope in God's gracious care.

It is wisdom and foolishness.

It is a hug and a warm bed.

It is emptiness when absent and frustration when home.

It is Kenner easy bake cookies and a cherry pie.

It is a source of meaning and a place for nonsense.

It is the Dallas Cowboys and Family Affair.

It is the death of a kitten and the beauty of a budding rose.

It is my family - God's gift to me.

Jim Dolby

ON THIS THANKSGIVING EVE

On this Thanksgiving Eve
I am grateful for our nation
A nation which has given me the opportunity to choose
The choice to worship -- or not
The choice to study -- or not
The choice to rise above the common place things -- or to
    rationalize my place in society and be miserable

I like to think that this country means more to me
Than simply material wealth and personal comfort
Yet, I choose to corrupt my children
With things they do not need and often do not want
This is my choice
For which I thank God
Knowing full well that the proper perspective must be faced at a
    future date

I am grateful to live in a country
Where independent thought is encouraged
And practiced to an almost overwhelming confusion
I thank God for my country
Where an experiment in mass education continues
Where knowledge gained is so great
That the individual almost becomes hysterical at its mass
I thank God for a country
Where a few dedicated men are willing to give their lives
In defense of the great majority
And the Mother suffers for her lifetime

I thank God for my country
Its strengths and its weaknesses alike
For, like each of its individual citizens
It lives and breathes
Smiles and cries
Is happy and sad

For all of this
I am glad and grateful to God
On this Thanksgiving Eve.

Bob Johnson

90

TABLE PRAYERS

Kind heavenly Father
We pause to recognize Thee as Lord and Master
Make us truly thankful for our food.
May we realize that every table where man meets to partake of
food is Thy communion table.
Help us to feel thy love and the love of our fellow man.
Give us eyes to see thy beauty and an understanding which will
enable us to accept change.

And, O Lord God, grant us the wisdom to know that thy
creation is good,
And that thy divinely constituted laws must and will prevail.

Jamie Smith Davis

Kind heavenly Father
We thank thee for food and thy many blessings which daily
surround us.
In today's rapid, changing, advancing, vacillating world, enable
each of us to find our right place of service.

As Autumn approaches,
Grant us eyes to see beauty
Ears to hear music
And hearts to feel not only thy love
But the love of our fellow man.

Jamie Smith Davis

A Time to Remember

"This is my commandment, that you love one another as I have loved you."

John 15:12

Lake Shore Baptist Church was born in December 1959. Each year on the first Sunday of December we give thanks for the community we have been ... now are ... will become. It is an altogether human fellowship, marked by frustration and fulfillment ... hurts and hopes ... failure and forgiveness. It is not the community for which we hope and pray and work, but here and there it has signs of being the People of God.

Whatever else you say about the community, it is a "church that love built" and is building. One of our members wrote the song which we sing on our anniversary Sunday and on other special occasions -- "The Church That Love Built."

"A Charge to the Church" reflects the hard word the church hears. It speaks of the painful and inevitable task to which we are called. "A Prayer for the Church" reminds us of the unity of our diverse community. "From the Desk of a Dove" is a reflection on our first decade.

THE CHURCH THAT LOVE BUILT

This is the church that love built;
Built as a haven for man --
Deep in our hearts we felt a need,
And a miracle happened from that small seed.
God brought these people together,
To further His wonderful plan --
Now to the stranger within our walls,
We open our hearts and extend love's call;
For we know there's a special place for all,
In the wonderful church that love built.

This is the church that love built,
Born of God's purpose for man.
God sent us Jesus, that we might see
Perfect love is the power that sets men free.
God built this Body eternal,
The church was His ultimate plan.
This is the mission we must fulfill,
To show that the church is an army still,
Marching forth with the power to do His will
As a part of the church that love built.

This is the church redemptive,
Firmly, forever it stands,
Giving assurance to every man
That eternal salvation is God's own plan.
This is the torch we must carry,
Gladly we offer our hands.
Now we must follow His great command,
To carry the word into every land,
For we must be a part of God's great band
In the wonderful church that love built.

Penny Edens

A CHARGE TO THE CHURCH: BE A GADFLY

As early as the 5th century B.C.
And as recently at the 20th century A.D.
Creative spirits have referred to themselves as gadflies.

In the 5th century B.C.
Socrates did so from an Athenian street.
In the 20th century A.D.
Martin Luther King did so from a Birmingham jail.
It was the purpose of the former to sting the minds of men
Stimulating them to creative thought.
It was the purpose of the latter to sting the hearts of men
Stimulating them to creative action.

It is the purpose of the Church to do both

What an awesome responsibility to be a gadfly!
But then we are the Church of Jesus Christ
And there has been no greater gadfly of the mind and heart
Than that peculiar One.

Robert Baird

A PRAYER FOR THE CHURCH

My body is the church
And all its parts, the whole.
I pray now for my body
As for my eternal soul,
As for my eternal soul.

My body is the church,
And I love every part.
I grieve to lose my smallest toe
As I grieve to lose my heart,
As I grieve to lose my heart.

And should my hand be cut from me
How I would feel the pain!
And I would feel the aching loss
'Til my arm be whole again,
'Til my arm be whole again.

Oh body, part of Christ,
I pray for you today
That He who is the Head of all
Will guide us on our way,
Will guide us on our way.

Penny Edens

FROM THE DESK OF --
A DOVE

Dear Lake Shore ...
　　　as of now ten years
Been filled with much laughter
　　　Been filled with some tears

With Peace and Love
　　　deep in our hearts
Lake Shore began
　　　with this good start

We strived for deep meaning
　　　and purpose of life
This came so easy
　　　with Bill and his wife

"Koinonia" and "agape"
　　　words here to stay
Stemmed from the hearts
　　　of Annetta and Rhea

"Being and becoming"
　　　part of God's revelation
Deryl offers to all
　　　in this great congregation

All of these people
　　　and many, many more
Help make a church
　　　we love and adore

So let us celebrate life
　　　as given and good!
It's ours for the taking
　　　And all of us should.

　　　　　　　Dot Martin

A Time for Christmas

"Prepare the way of the Lord..."

Isaiah 40:3

"Good news of a great joy which will come to all the people"

Luke 2:10

Christmas comes but once a year, but what a "once" it is. So much to do and see, to sing and be. The Church begins the Christmas celebration with Advent and continues for four weeks. It celebrates with tinsel and trees ... with parties and gifts ... with worship and calls to awareness ... with glad greetings and cries for help.

"Can Christmas Come?" picks up all the themes. It was written by a teacher as a Christmas greeting to her Sunday School class.

CAN CHRISTMAS COME?

"Can Christmas Come?" ... the preacher asked ...
    In words that rang so bold.
They stirred the heart that heard them ...
    On a wintry day so cold.

Can "Joy to the World" be heard this year ...
    O're the sound of the 6 o'clock news?
And even if we manage to hear the words ...
    Can the "Joy" overcome the blues?

These nights are far from silent ...
    There's shopping each night 'til nine ...
Hurry! the voices remind us ...
    Rush! ... There's so little time!

    There are presents to buy ... but the prices so high!
    There are packages to mail ... and the wreath to nail!
    There are the cookies to bake ... and those favors to
      make!
    The tree is too small ... and there's no time at all!

    Oh, the list is much too long ...
    And I'm too tired to hear the angel's song.

Can Christmas Come? I ask myself ...
    In our world where hearts are cold ...
Where every home has become a marketplace ...
    Where men are bought and sold?

If Christmas comes ... can it come to all ...
    Or to only a chosen few?
Will every hungry, dirty child ...
    See it with me and you?

In my heart, I know the answer ...
    And it hurts ... but I know its true ...
Christmas can come only as the love of God ...
    Is born again in *me* and *you!*

Merry Christmas!

Minnie Herring

100

A Time for Us

"For everything there is a season ..."

Indeed there is a time for everything in the life of the People of God. If we are to celebrate any of life, we must celebrate all of it. We have learned to trust God to break the darkness with the dawn, the cold winter with the crisp spring, the season of despair with the season of hope.

So we share a year of our soul stirrings that reflects what any year is for the Community of Faith. "Seasons" was written by one of our children.

Ours is a Life of Faith -- not certainty, safety, security -- but Faith. Out of the ashes of one dream comes another, as "Dream's End" suggests.

SEASONS

The grass turned green

        as it started to grow,

The sun shone forth

        with golden glow.

Then winter came,

        the grass turned brown,

Behind the clouds

        the sun went down.

But springtime came,

        God sent the rain,

Flowers bloomed

        and robins sang.

Then summer appeared

        and fun time was here.

And now what has passed?

        Another year.

            Debby Campbell

DREAM'S END

Oh Camelot, I hear your wondrous story,
See your shining glory on the screen.
Cry as all about you turns to ashes,
Noble hopes reduced to empty dream.

But do I cry for you, oh noble Arthur,
For Lancelot or tragic Guinevere?
Do I cry for noble aspirations
Doomed because of jealousy and fear?

Oh no, I cry for quite a different reason,
For I too had a Camelot one day.
But like a fool I didn't even know it
'Til helplessly I watched it slip away.

Oh would that I had somehow found the secret
To keep that perfect time, but I did not.
And now I know that God did not intend it
Man was not meant to live in Camelot.

Penny Edens

Epilogue

So we, the People of God, dream the impossible dream. And we sense enough reality to go on dreaming and daring. And we share our dreams with one another in worship, study, fellowship, and now in writing.

This "sounding forth" of ours calls to mind the celebration of another in the long line of "the communion of the saints," the Apostle Paul:

> "I thank my God in all my remembrance of you, always in every prayer of mine for you all making my prayer with joy, thankful for your partnership in the gospel from the first day until now" (Philippians 1:3-5).

Celebrants

Robert Baird - professor of philosophy, husband and father

Darla Barrett - sophomore in high school, pianist, babysitter

Daryl Barrett - college sophomore with architectural aspirations

Gary Don Boyd - the church's Minister of Youth, college senior, poet, ministerial student

Susan Brister - 7th grader, middle child with two sisters and two brothers

Buzz Brown - college freshman with unusual balance of academic, athletic, social and spiritual concerns

Mary Brown - mother of four, high school English teacher, adult Sunday School teacher

Debby Campbell - 7th grader who is already well organized

Charlotte Carpenter - mother of five, poet, creative and versatile at church and in the community

Kathy Casner - 6th grader with many interests

Bobby Cunningham - college senior, honor student, ministerial inclinations

Jamie Smith Davis - retired school teacher, an older "young spirit"

Jim Dolby - father of four girls, psychologist, writer, deacon

Penny Edens - wife, mother and grandmother, children's choir director, the church's poet and playwright

Beverly Fleming - mother and wife, college Sunday School teacher

Deryl Fleming - Pastor of the church, husband, father and editor of this book

Carolyn Henson - wife and mother of two girls, the church's Elementary Director

Jerry Henson - the church's Minister of Education, graduate student, husband and father

Minnie Herring - wife, mother, bookkeeper, Sunday School teacher

Beverly Hill - kindergarten teacher, wife, mother of two girls, poet

Stella Osgood Humphrey - deceased member of the church after a rich life as wife and mother and a distinguished career of college and church teaching

Bart Jenkins - 9th grader, avid sports fan

Bob Johnson - public school administrator, husband and father, deacon and Sunday School teacher

Barbara Johnston - wife, mother of three boys, social worker, church choir director

Kathy Kolar - college junior, pursuing psychology and children's work

Dot Martin - secretary of the church, mother and wife

Vicki Martin - college freshman, daughter and sister, charmer

Donna McMullen - mother, wife, poet

Hugh McMullen - engineer, husband, father, Sunday School teacher of 6th grade boys, deacon

Bob Wayne Ousley - beginning a career in the arts, accomplished musician and actor

Alton Pearson - hospital administrator, husband and father of three sons, distinguished in service to the church and the community

Ron Smith - college professor, Ph.D. candidate in religion, husband and father of four

Julie Spain - high school junior, musician

George Williams - salesman, father and husband, deacon

Jan Williams - wife and mother, Sunday School teacher, choir soloist

Special Thanks

To Dot Martin
      for typing, proofing and motivating
To John Cook
      whose men and machines did the job
To Dennis Hill
      who designed the cover
To Mary Ruth Howse
      for editorial suggestions